Slippy's journey home.

Written & illustrated
by Steven Dibley

Hi I'm Slippy, I'm going
home.

"S S S S S S S S S S S"
Said Slippy

Slippy slithered across the grass
on his way home.

Now .... Slippy is a slithery, snake.

"SSSSSsₛˢsss"
Said Slippy

Slippy slithered across the grass and went through a puddle on his way home.

Now ……. Slippy is a wet, slippery, slithery, snake.

"SSSSSsSsss"

Said Slippy

Slippy slithered across the grass, went through a puddle and some leaves on his way home.

Now .... Slippy is a seriously leafy, wet, slippery, slithery, snake.

"sSSSSsSsss"

Said Slippy

Slippy slithered across the grass, went through a puddle and some leaves, then through some paint on his way home .

Now .... Slippy is a spotty, paint covered, seriously leafy, wet, slippery, slithery, snake.

"SSSSSsₛSₛSS"

Said Slippy

Slippy slithered across the grass, went through a puddle and some leaves, then through some paint and managed to fit through a fence on his way home.

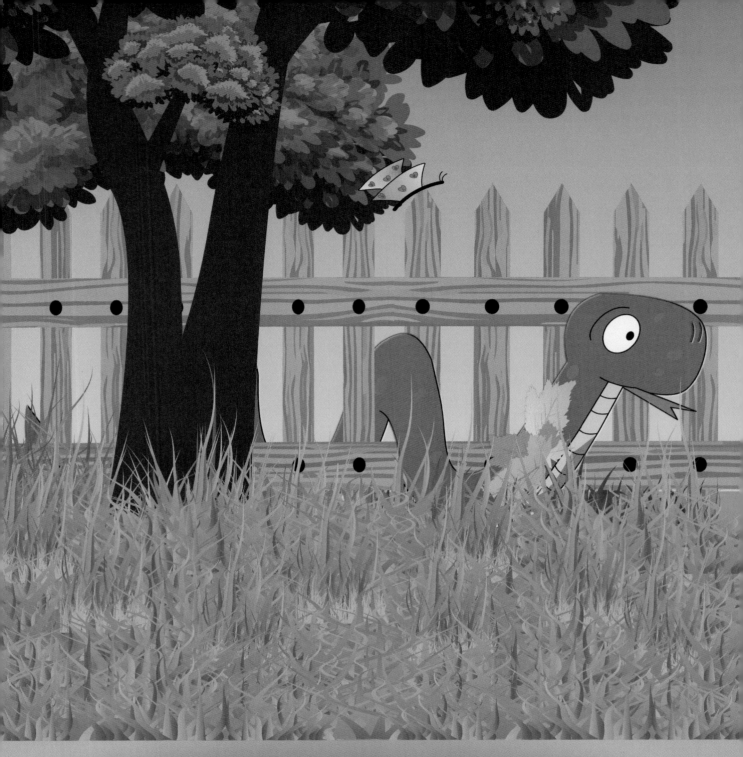

Now .... Slippy is a skinny, spotty, paint covered, seriously leafy, wet, slippery, slithery, snake.

"SSSSSsSSss"

Said Slippy

Slippy slithered across the grass, went through a puddle and some leaves, then through some paint and managed to fit through a fence, he also had to sneak past some foxes while passing their den on his way home.

Now .... Slippy is a sneaky, skinny, spotty, paint covered, seriously leafy, wet, slippery, slithery, snake.

"SSSSSs$_s$^{s}ss"

Said Slippy

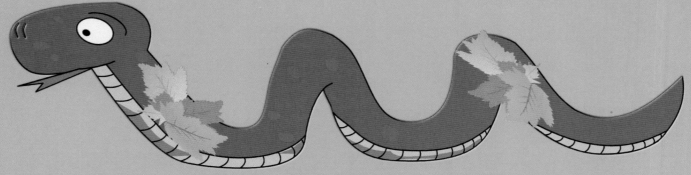

Slippy slithered across the grass, went through a puddle and some leaves, then through some paint and managed to fit through a fence, he also had to sneak past some foxes while passing their den, then had to be super quiet passing baby birds on his way home.

Now .... Slippy is a super silent, sneaky, skinny, spotty, paint covered, seriously leafy, wet, slippery, slithery, snake.

"SSSSSₛˢₛSS"

Said Slippy

Slippy slithered across the grass, went through a puddle and some leaves, then through some paint and managed to fit through a fence, he also had to sneak past some foxes while passing their den, then had to be super quiet passing baby birds, he was now feeling awesome as he was nearly home.

Now .... Slippy is an awesomely, super silent, sneaky, skinny, spotty, paint covered, seriously leafy, wet, slippery, slithery, snake.

"SSSSSₛˢₛss"
Said Slippy

Slippy slithered across the grass, went through a puddle and some leaves, then through some paint and managed to fit through a fence, he also had to sneak past some foxes while passing their den, then had to be super quiet passing baby birds, he was now feeling awesome but could hear something coming so he moved really fast on his way home.

Now .... Slippy is a supersonic fast moving, awesomely, super silent, sneaky, skinny, spotty, paint covered, seriously leafy, wet, slippery, slithery, snake.

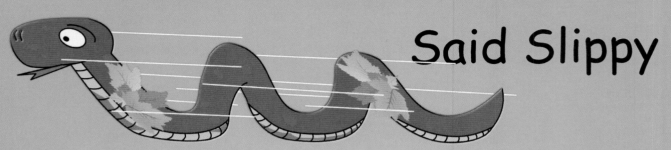

"ssSsSsₛSₛSss"

Said Slippy

Slippy slithered across the grass, went through a puddle and some leaves, then through some paint and managed to fit through a fence, he also had to sneak past some foxes while passing their den, then had to be super quiet passing baby birds, he was now feeling awesome but could hear something coming so he moved really fast, then with a great big smile, Slippy was home at last.

Now .... Slippy is a big smiling, supersonic, fast moving, awesomely, super silent, sneaky, skinny, spotty, paint covered, seriously leafy, wet, slippery, slithery, snake.

"SSSSSsSSSS"

Said Slippy

THE END

Printed in Great Britain
by Amazon